The Sun, the Wind, and Tashira

A Hottentot Tale from Africa

Retold by Elizabeth Claire
Illustrated by Elise Mills

Folklore Consultant: Bette Bosma

MONDO Publishing
One Plaza Road
Greenvale, New York 11548

Copyright © 1994, 1992 by Mondo Publishing
EXPANDED EDITION 1994

Printed in the United States of America
94 95 96 97 98 99   9 8 7 6 5 4 3 2 1

Photograph/Illustration Credits Jason Laure: pp. 17, 20; Nigel Dennis/Photo
Researchers: p. 18; U. D. Transvaal, Cape Colony/The New York Public Library
Picture Collection: p. 19; Patrick Frilet/Sipa: p. 21 top; Van der Hilst/Liaison
International: p. 21 bottom.

Library of Congress Cataloging-in-Publication Data

Claire, Elizabeth.
     The sun, the wind, and Tashira : a Hottentot tale from Africa / retold by Elizabeth
Claire ; illustrated by Elise Mills.
          p.   cm.
     Summary: The sun and the wind try to please a young girl by bringing colors into
her life in the dry and dusty place where she lives in southern Africa.
     ISBN 1-879531-08-9 : $21.95. — ISBN 1-879531-41-0 : $9.95. —
ISBN 1-879531-20-8 : $4.95
     [1. Folklore, Khoikhoi. 2. Folklore—Africa, Southern.]   I. Mills, Elise, ill.
II. Title. III. Series.
PZ8.1.C49Su   1994
398.26—dc20
[E]   94-8129
                                                                                                CIP
                                                                                                 AC

As a child I often begged my parents to spin a tale for me, but it wasn't until I grew up that I realized how important storytelling is in my African American culture. The story of Tashira brings back memories of the tales I heard as a child. I see myself and my culture in the pictures. Read on and discover the tale for yourself.

Beth Smith

Tashira lived in a dry and dusty land. Her mother, the Queen of Fountains, worked all day bringing water for the young corn.

When Tashira found a tiny yellow flower, a pretty orange stone or a bright red berry, she was happy. That made her mother happy too.

Tashira loved colors more than anything. One day, the Sun painted the sky a beautiful blue. "I did this for you," said the Sun.

"Thank you," said Tashira.

She lay under the Baobab tree and looked at the blue sky. The Sun was glad...but the Wind was jealous.

Soon after that, the Wind brought clouds to the dry land. He made them drop their rain. Millions of flowers bloomed.

"I did this for you," said the Wind.

"Thank you," said Tashira.

She danced in the green grass. She made necklaces from violets. She put red and yellow flowers in her hair.

The Wind was very angry. "Is that all you can say?" He flew into a rage. He blew down the young corn. He blew the green grass away. He blew the beautiful flowers off their stems.

Tashira was very sad. All the colors
were gone.

The land was dry and dusty
again. Tashira lay down
under her Baobab tree and
stared at the only color left:
the blue sky.

That evening, the Sun painted new colors in the sky. Tashira climbed the highest hill to look at them. The Sun tried more colors every evening, and Tashira was happy again.

One day, Tashira told her mother, "I want to live in the sky with the Sun." So her mother told all the animals and people to help make a tall ladder.

The ladder went up into the sky.
Tashira climbed and climbed.

Suddenly there was a horrible sound.

It was the Wind. He was furious. He blew so hard that stones flew. Crackkkk. Down came the ladder. And down came Tashira.

Then the Wind became very quiet. Tashira's mother cried and cried. Her tears fell on Tashira and made a soft cloud around her.

The cloud carried
Tashira up, up, up.
The Sun touched the
cloud and suddenly
    there were beautiful
    colors all over the sky.
    Tashira had become a
    rainbow.

All over the world, people use stories to explain how the wonders of nature were created. *The Sun, the Wind, and Tashira* is one of these tales told by the Hottentot people of Africa.

Homes like those of the Hottentots.

Creation tales are told in many countries. The Micmac Indians of Canada tell about how summer came to their country. In the United States, the Ojibway tell stories about star maidens who came to Earth and became water lilies. In Greece, stories about the goddess of the harvest explain why there are four seasons. And people all over China tell a tale about why the Milky Way is in the sky.

Dry, bare desert of southwest Africa.

Paintings of African animals.

In *The Sun, the Wind, and Tashira*, the artist shows how dry and bare the land is and how the rains change it for a short time. The houses have the special shape the Hottentots used for their homes long ago. Most of the animals shown lived only in Africa, and people often painted pictures of them on rocks.

The Hottentots lived in the desert and plains of southwest Africa. They raised cattle and moved often to find food. Today, descendants of the Hottentots are called Namas, and the part of Africa where they lived is the country Namibia. The Namas live there with people from other African groups, and each group has its own language.

In small villages and cities, two languages are used in school. Children learn in their own language and in English.

Schoolchildren having fun.

Child helping at a cattle ranch.

Today, cattle and sheep are raised on large ranches. Land in desert areas is supplied with water so crops can grow there. Many village people work at wildlife preserves where wild animals such as elephants, giraffes, and zebras are protected. Visitors from all over travel to Namibia to see the animals.

Elephants in a wildlife preserve